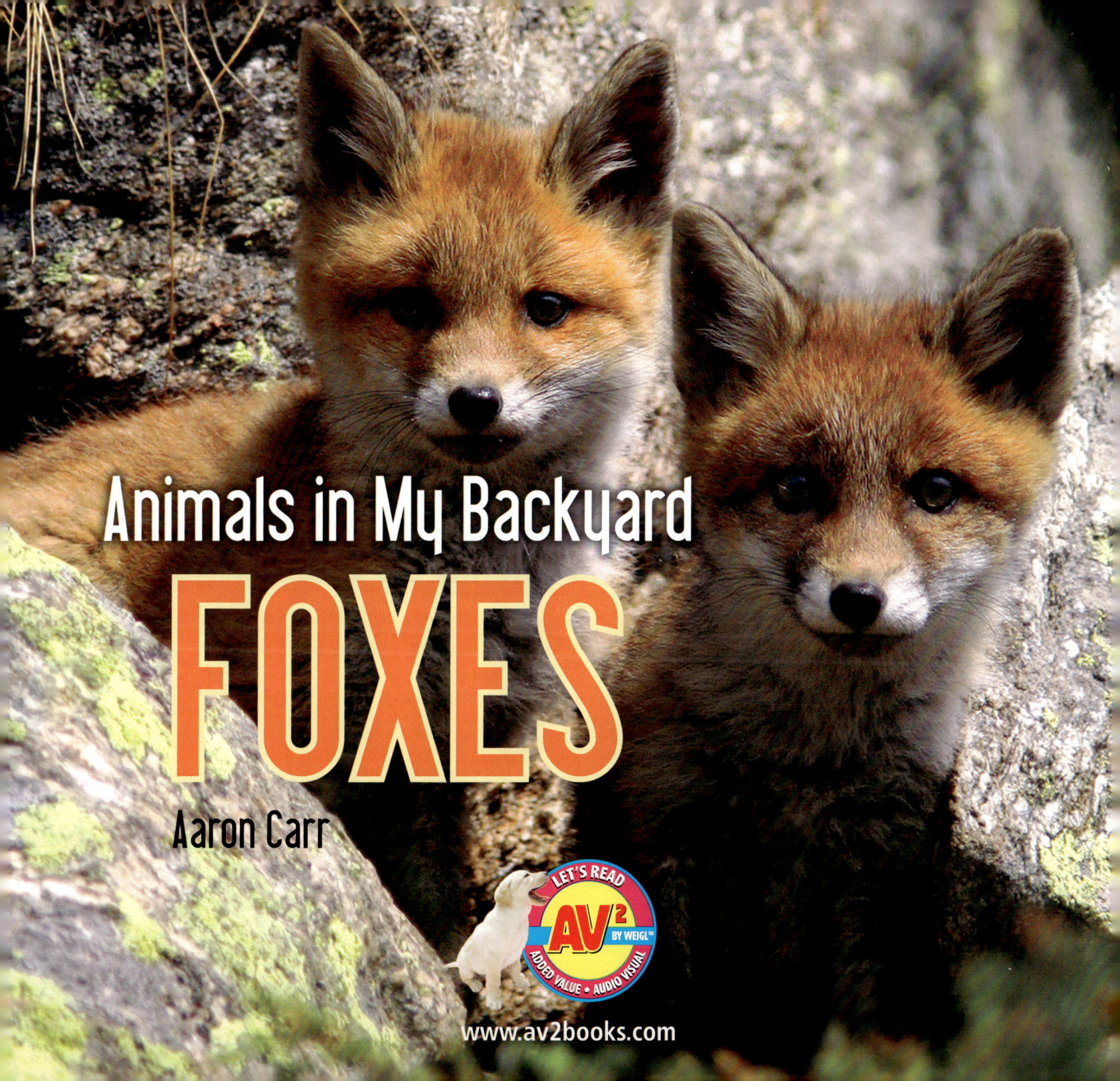

Animals in My Backyard

FOXES

Aaron Carr

LET'S READ
AV²
BY WEIGL™
ADDED VALUE • AUDIO VISUAL

Go to **www.av2books.com**, and enter this book's unique code.

BOOK CODE

H596273

AV² by Weigl brings you media enhanced books that support active learning.

AV² provides enriched content that supplements and complements this book. Weigl's AV² books strive to create inspired learning and engage young minds in a total learning experience.

Your AV² Media Enhanced books come alive with...

Audio
Listen to sections of the book read aloud.

Key Words
Study vocabulary, and complete a matching word activity.

Video
Watch informative video clips.

Quizzes
Test your knowledge.

Embedded Weblinks
Gain additional information for research.

Slide Show
View images and captions, and prepare a presentation.

Try This!
Complete activities and hands-on experiments.

... and much, much more!

Published by AV² by Weigl.
350 5th Avenue, 59th Floor New York, NY 10118
Websites: www.av2books.com   www.weigl.com

Library of Congress Cataloging-in-Publication Data
Carr, Aaron.
 Foxes / Aaron Carr.
    pages cm. -- (Animals in my backyard)
 Includes index.
 ISBN 978-1-4896-2942-5 (hard cover : alk. paper) -- ISBN 978-1-4896-2943-2 (soft cover : alk. paper) -- ISBN 978-1-4896-2944-9 (single user ebook)
-- ISBN 978-1-4896-2945-6 (multi-user ebook)
 1. Foxes--Juvenile literature. I. Title.
 QL737.C22C368 2016
 599.775--dc23
                                2014039095

Printed in the United States of America in Brainerd, Minnesota
1 2 3 4 5 6 7 8 9 0 18 17 16 15 14

122014
WEP051214

Project Coordinator: Heather Kissock   Designer: Mandy Christiansen

Weigl acknowledges Getty Images and iStock as the primary image suppliers for this title.

Animals in My Backyard
FOXES

CONTENTS

Meet the fox.

She looks like a pet dog.

She lives with her family when she is young.

When she is young, her mother and father take care of her.

She can run fast with her long, thin legs.

With her long, thin legs,
she can jump very high.

She uses her long tail to stay warm.

To stay warm, she wraps her tail around her body like a blanket.

She talks with yips, howls, and growls.

With yips, howls, and growls, she can find other foxes.

She hears with her large, pointed ears.

With her large, pointed ears, she can find animals under the ground.

She hunts mostly at night.

At night, she tracks other animals like a cat.

She can be found in many parts of the world.

In many parts of the world, she lives in the forest.

If you meet the fox, she may be afraid. She might run from you.

If you meet the fox, stay away.

FOX FACTS

These pages provide more detail about the interesting facts found in the book. They are intended to be used by adults as a learning support to help young readers round out their knowledge of each animal featured in the *Animals in My Backyard* series.

Pages 4–5

A fox looks like a pet dog. As part of the canine family, foxes are closely related to domestic dogs. There are about 10 species of fox. The smallest of these species is the fennec fox, which measures about 28 inches (72 centimeters) in length. The red fox is the largest species. It can be about 56 inches (142 cm) in length.

Pages 6–7

Foxes live with their families when they are young. A female fox makes a special room in her den before she gives birth. This room is called a nesting chamber. After a gestation period of about 53 days, she gives birth to as many as 13 babies, or pups. The mother and father both help to care for the pups.

Pages 8–9

Foxes have long, thin legs. Relative to their size, foxes tend to have longer, thinner legs than other members of the canine family. Having long rear legs gives the fox additional power in sprinting and jumping. A fox can reach speeds up to 45 miles (72 km) per hour. It can jump as high as 6.5 feet (2 meters).

Pages 10–11

Foxes have long tails. A fox's tail can be up to 22 inches (56 cm) long. The tail serves three main purposes. When running, jumping, and climbing, it acts as a counterweight to help keep the fox balanced. The thick, bushy fur also makes it a good blanket in cold weather. A fox will often wrap its tail around itself to stay warm. Foxes also use their tails to communicate their moods to other foxes.

Pages 12–13

Foxes use a variety of sounds to communicate. Like other canines, foxes are vocal animals. They communicate with one another using up to 28 different sounds, including barks, yips, howls, and growls. Foxes can recognize other foxes based on the sounds of their voices. This allows them to connect with family and stay away from rivals. Foxes also communicate using facial expressions and scent markings.

Pages 14–15

Foxes have excellent hearing. The fox has large, pointed ears positioned on the top of its head. These ears help the fox to pick up faint sounds. A fox can hear a watch tick from 40 yards (37 meters) away. Foxes can also hear low-pitched sounds that humans cannot hear. This helps them track animals that are moving underground.

Pages 16–17

Foxes are active mostly at night. Foxes have eyes that have adapted to see better in low light, like a cat's eyes. This, combined with their excellent hearing and smell, helps them hunt at night. Foxes hunt small animals such as rodents, rabbits, and birds. Unlike other canines, foxes stay low to the ground and stalk their prey, like a cat.

Pages 18–19

Foxes are found in many parts of the world. They are found in North America, Europe, Africa, Asia, and Australia. Although not considered true foxes, six additional fox-like species are found in South America. Foxes have one of the largest ranges of any land mammal. They prefer to make their homes in forests, but can also inhabit grasslands, deserts, and mountains.

Pages 20–21

Foxes are often found near places where people live. They are normally only a danger to humans when they have rabies, which is rare. Foxes tend to run away when a person approaches and are best left alone. Making loud noises, such as yelling or whistling, can scare off foxes that do not leave on their own.

23

KEY WORDS

Research has shown that as much as 65 percent of all written material published in English is made up of 300 words. These 300 words cannot be taught using pictures or learned by sounding them out. They must be recognized by sight. This book contains 46 common sight words to help young readers improve their reading fluency and comprehension. This book also teaches young readers several important content words. These words are paired with pictures to aid in learning and improve understanding.

Page	Sight Words First Appearance
4	the
5	a, like, looks, she
6	and, family, father, her, is, lives, mother, of, take, when, with, young
8	can, long, run
9	high, very
10	to, uses
11	around
12	talks
13	find, other
14	hears, large
15	animals, under
16	at, night
18	be, found, in, many, parts, world
20	away, from, if, may, might, you

Page	Content Words First Appearance
4	fox
5	dog
8	legs
10	tail
11	blanket, body
12	growls, howls, yips
14	ears
15	ground
16	cat
19	forest

Check out www.av2books.com for activities, videos, audio clips, and more!

1 Go to www.av2books.com.

2 Enter book code. H 5 9 6 2 7 3

3 Fuel your imagination online!

www.av2books.com